Brutus and the Relay Race

Dyslexic Friendly Edition

TIF E. BOOTS

Illustrated by Syranity Barker

DF Version ISBN-13: 978-1-963272-28-4

ShelteringTree.Earth, LLC
PO Box 973, Eagle Lake, FL 33839

ShelteringTreeMedia.com

What is a "Dyslexic Friendly" Book?

Sheltering Tree Media has taken steps to make our books more friendly for those who live with dyslexia. While the following principles will not make every book readable for every reader, it is our best effort to create products that encourage reading and to support all readers.

Throughout the book, we use a font named OpenDyslexic. This is a free font that is designed to help dyslexic readers distinguish each letter from the others. For more information about OpenDyslexic, how it differs from other fonts, and research behind the font, visit their website: www.opendyslexic.com.

In our books created for children, we use a font size which provides the reader with plenty of spacing between the letters (which is called *kerning*). The bigger, wider font tends to be easier to the reader's eyes.

The space between each word is increased (this is called *word spacing*). This helps better to distinguish when one word ends and the next begins. The line spacing is greater than most common fonts (this is called *leading*). This all should help with readability.

Whenever possible, the text is Left-Aligned but it is not justified on the right side. Allowing the right side of a paragraph to remain *rough* keeps the word spacing consistent throughout.

Our Dyslexic Friendly books are printed on cream or ivory paper which is also thicker than the average book page. This minimizes the sharp contrast of black-on-white pages as well as bleedthrough of text from the previous page.

Finally, Sheltering Tree Media has made colored overlays available when you purchase a book through our online store. You can find these overlays at ShelteringTreeMedia.com/shop/dyslexic-friendly.

These are some of the principles we use to create a book as readable as possible to those living with dyslexia. Some may find this helpful; some may not. Please provide us with any insights you might have to improve our Dyslexic Friendly principles. We pray this will enable many to heighten their love for reading.

DEDICATION

For all the people who have been a part of
my life.

BRUTUS and the RELAY RACE

Charlie was super excited and couldn't wait for the sun to rise. He poked his head out of the drey again.

"What are you doing?" asked his mom. "Are you trying to shake the whole nest?"

"I'm sorry, Mom." Charlie said, "the sun is taking too long to rise. My friends and I are planning a relay race today!"

"You keep circling inside the nest and you won't have the energy to run a race." His mom laughed, "The sun will rise when it is time. Until then sit down and have something to eat before your race."

Charlie tried to calm down and eat but after every bite she saw him looking towards the door.

Finally the sun started to shine brightly and lit up the nest. Charlie dashed out the door and down the branches into the tree.

He was almost to the bottom branch when he heard Brutus call for Scrump. He raced down the trunk of the tree just as Scrump crawled out of his burrow.

"Good Morning," Charlie called. "I am so excited for the race today. I could not even sleep last night. Are we ready to start? I can't wait to race today." Charlie chittered too fast for anyone one else to say anything.

"Charlie?"

The friends heard a small whisper from above when Charlie finally stopped talking to take a breath. Looking up they saw a small grey head with bright purple eyes looking down at them.

BRUTUS and the RELAY RACE

"Colleen, What are you doing here?" Charlie asked his little sister.

"Mama says I am big enough to leave the nest without her as long as I am with you or stay close to the tree," Colleen explained. "You were so excited about the race today. I wanted to ask if I can play, too."

Charlie looked to Brutus and Scrump for an answer.

"It's okay with us," said Brutus. "You can't have a relay race with only one team."

"That's true," agreed Scrump. "We need to find more friends."

Just then they heard a small voice squeak behind them. They all turned to see a little brown and white hedgehog with black eyes and pointy hair.

"Hello," said the hedgehog in her small squeaky voice, "I'm Henrietta. I did not mean to eavesdrop, but if you are looking for someone to play, can I join in the race?"

"Of course you can," Scrump answered. "How about we split up and see who else wants to play? We can meet back here and go over the rules."

"Sounds like a plan," agreed Brutus and Charlie and off the three of them ran, leaving Colleen and Henrietta by themselves at the tree.

Colleen climbed down the tree and sat in front of Henrietta.

"My mom says if I'm not with Charlie, I am too young to go too far away from the tree," she explained to her new friend.

"My mom says I am too young to go far from the barn by myself, too." Henrietta suggested, "How about we stay here and greet everyone that comes?"

"That's a good idea," said a new voice. "I would like to play, too, but my mom also says I am too young to go too far from our nest."

Colleen and Henrietta both jumped in surprise and looked around to see a young racoon peeking around the corner of the barn at them.

"This is also my first time out without my mom. I am happy to meet other animals my age."

When Brutus returned to the tree, he was surprised to find Colleen and Henrietta talking to a small racoon. Before he could introduce himself, he saw Dash, Lawrence, Twitter, Patches, Scrump, and Charlie all running or flying towards them.

"Wow!" Colleen laughed. "I did not know I would meet so many new friends today."

"Well, we have some new faces here today," observed Dash. "Maybe we should start with names."

"I'm Jack," said the racoon. "This is Colleen and Henrietta. I hope it does not ruin the race but our moms say we are too young to go very far from our nests still."

"If it will hurt the race," Henrietta added, "we can play something else while you guys race."

"I think we can work with that," said Lawrence.

"Yes," agreed Patches. "You guys can run the last part of the race that way you are closest to the tree."

"I will be flying above as a judge," said Twitter. " I am not made for running and it would not be fair if I flew. So I will be able to keep an eye on everyone, too."

After introductions, the new friends came up with rules and the lay out of the race.

"I think," Dash began. "To keep the race as close to fair as we can, that Lawrence, Brutus, and I should all be on separate teams. We have an advantage since we are bigger and have longer legs."

"I agree," said Scrump. "You guys can be the team captains and the younger ones can chose whose team they want to be on and run the last part of the race."

Colleen went over and stood next to Brutus.

Henrietta chose to be on Lawrence's team.

"Well Jack, I guess that means you are stuck with me," teased Dash.

Scrump, Charlie, and Patches were left to choose the teams they wanted.

Charlie thought it would be best if he and Colleen were on different teams. That way, they both had a better chance of being on a winning team. He chose to stand with Lawrence and Henrietta.

Scrump liked running against Brutus, sometimes Brutus was clumsy and tripped when he ran. Scrump was usually always able to catch up if Brutus was having a clumsy day. So Scrump went over to stand with Dash and Jack.

That left Patches to race with Brutus and Colleen.

"Okay," she said. "It looks like the teams are pretty even. What are the rules of the race?"

"I found a couple of sticks this morning. They are going to be our relay items," explained Brutus. "We start here and have to carry the stick all the way to the slide, where we pass it to our next teammate. They will run it to the next member of the team at the tractor my owners left by the field of tall grass."

"From there, they will pass it to the last teammate who will then run it back to the tree. First team to get their stick back here and put it down next to the tree trunk wins."

"That is a good route," said Twitter. "But I do see a small problem with it. Charlie and Henrietta, will you each pick up a stick and try to run with it?"

Charlie and Henrietta both tried to pick up a stick but each of them were too big for them to carry. Patches and Scrump also tried, and the sticks were too long and fat for them to carry without tripping.

"Oh," said Brutus. "I didn't think that some of us may not be able to carry those. What should we do?"

"Twitter, can you find some smaller sticks and maybe some that are more of a medium size?" asked Lawrence.

"I sure can! I just saw some this morning. I'll be right back." She ruffled her wings to take off.

"How about we have to put our sticks at the top of the slide, and the next set can not pick up their sticks until we slide down and tag our partner?" suggested Dash.

"Oh, that would be fun," agreed Brutus. "I like the slide."

Soon Twitter returned. "I put three medium sticks near the bottom of the slide and three small sticks by the tractor near the grass field. During the race, I will fly over the field and announce what is happening, so that the animals waiting know what is going on."

"I think we are ready to race then!" exclaimed Charlie.

"Everyone to your starting points!" said Twitter. "When everyone is ready, I will shriek to begin the race."

"I am going to walk the path with the little ones before I go to the slide," said Scrump. "We don't want them getting lost on their first trip away from the nest."

Brutus, Dash and Lawrence took their places sitting with the sticks at their feet and waited for Twitter's call to start the race.

Scrump, Charlie, and Patches all walked the little ones back to the tractor and made sure they were ready. Once the little ones were all set and comfortable with the race route, they headed back to the slide.

"Remember," Twitter called from above. "You can not pick up your stick or run until your partner has made it down the slide, put their stick down, and tagged you."

They all nodded.

Twitter flew off to check on the younger animals. "You can't pick up your sticks to run until your teammate drops theirs and tags you," she reminded them. "I will be flying above to make sure no one gets lost."

Henrietta, Colleen and Jack all nodded and Twitter flew towards the larger animals. "On your marks," she called. "Get set. Go!!!" She shrieked loud enough for everyone to hear.

Brutus, Dash and Lawrence all grabbed their sticks and took off. Lawrence quickly took the lead, a few strides later, Dash caught up. Then Brutus had a burst of energy and seemed to fly past them both.

Brutus was running so fast and he could see the slide. He glanced over his shoulder as he ran. Dash and Lawrence were not very far behind him. He ran even faster.

Just a few feet from the slide, Brutus's feet got ahead of him and he tripped over his own paws. He rolled head over tail until the slide stopped him suddenly.

Lawrence jumped over him and onto the first step of the slide as Brutus rolled. Brutus shook his head and stood up as Dash started his climb up the slide. Lawrence and Dash both got to the top, dropped their sticks, and slid down.

Lawrence was down the slide first but missed his landing and had to run back to tag Charlie. Dash landed right in front of Scrump and tagged him just as Brutus hit the ground from his slide.

Twitter flew above the racers, yelling out for all to hear. "The race has started it looks like Lawrence is off to a quick start. Dash is coming in fast behind him. Oh! They are neck and neck! But wait where did Brutus come from? There he goes, he has passed them both and taken the lead."

"The slide is in sight, Lawrence and Dash are catching up, but Brutus seems to be unstoppable."

"Oh No! and we have a racer down. Brutus has tripped just steps away from the slide. Lawrence takes advantage and jumps past him. Dash is on his heels as they climb the steps. Brutus is up and climbing."

"The first stick is down, and Lawrence slides for the finish. Dash drops his stick and follows Lawrence down the slide. Oh... Lawrence missed the landing he passed his teammate. He is going to have to run back, and tag Charlie before Charlie is allowed to start."

"Dash tags Scrump, and Brutus has caught up and tagged Patches. Lawrence completed his portion of the race and tagged his teammate. Charlie can start." She recited loudly for the others to hear.

Scrump picked up his stick and turned to run. Lawrence tagged Charlie at the same time that Brutus tagged Patches.

Off they all ran: Scrump ahead by a nose, but Patches, having a slightly longer nose, quickly caught up.

Charlie bounded past them both, running a squirrelly zigzag in front of them. Scrump added a long jump to his run and took the lead.

The race was close, they all made it to the lawnmower and dropped their sticks at the same time. Patches tagged Colleen, Scrump tagged Jack, and Charlie tagged Henrietta.

"Off they go," Twitter shouted. "Scrump is a head by a nose, but Patches is quickly catching up. Here comes Charlie bounding past them both. His squirrelly zigzags seem to be confusing and slowing the other contestants down. Scrump springs over Charlie to take the lead. This is going to be a close race."

"Patches just gave a burst of speed, and they made it to the lawn mower. All sticks are down. Colleen, Jack and Henrietta have all been tagged and pick up their sticks.

The little ones picked up their sticks and were off at full speed.

Colleen dashed away and toward the oak tree. Jack was right behind her.

The ground sloped into a gentle hill. Henrietta ducked her head and turned her body into a pokey little ball. She quickly rolled past her friends. She slowed down slightly as the ground flattened out and untucked herself from the ball, shaking her head to clear the dizziness.

A chorus of chants and cheers filled the air as the racers approached.

In front of the barn with the tree just ahead, Jack and Colleen sped up and passed her. Jack took a deep breath and dove, sliding on his belly to the tree. Colleen made a long jump over him and onto the tree trunk. They both dropped their sticks as Henrietta reached the tree.

All was as quiet as a heartbeat as the onlookers waited for the sticks to land.

"Colleen has jumped into the lead, but Jack is right behind her as they head down the slope. What is this?! It seems Henrietta has a trick or two. She has turned herself into a ball and is rolling down the decline. I bet she's going to be dizzy before she finds the end."

Twitter continued to call the race. "Henrietta has the lead, but Jack and Colleen are making quick work and closing the distance. The crowd goes wild as Jack takes a dive, he slides on his belly to the tree. Colleen leaps onto the tree. Here's Henrietta still looking a little dizzy from her roll. Jack and Colleen drop their sticks. Who's will hit the ground first?"

"Wow," Brutus panted as the other racers gathered at the finish.

"That was some race!" agreed Dash.

"Who won?" asked Charlie.

Dash looked around at the crowd, "Where did everyone come from?"

Scrump looked at the animals that had gathered around to see the race. It looked like every animal they ever met had come out to watch the excitement. His mom and dad sat just outside of the burrow. In the tree above them was a couple of grey squirrels. A family of hedgehogs were standing with a family of racoons near the barn. Even Mr. Frog and Herbie the turtle had come.

91

Twitter fluttered up and landed on the branch with Charlie's parents. "That was a fantastic race!" She announced. "It was so close. We had a bunch of strong competitors. How about a cheer for all of our runners today?"

The crowd erupted into applause and cheering. When it quieted,Twitter continued, "The winning team for today's race was -- Jack, Scrump and Dash."

The crowd cheered even louder.

Henrietta and Colleen put their heads down and walked away.

Lawrence watched them go.

When the crowd started to clear out, Lawrence snuck away to the other side of the barn where he had seen the two younger animals go. "What is wrong?" he asked the girls when he found them. "Didn't you have fun today?"

"It was fun," said Henrietta. "But I really wanted to help my team win. We lost because I am too small."

"My team didn't win either," Colleen pouted.

Lawrence sighed, "Not everyone or every team can win every time. Winning is not nearly as important as having fun and trying your best. You guys both did great today."

"You missed the action at the slide when Brutus was in the lead and tripped. Or when I was in the lead and slid right past Charlie. I lost the lead when I had to run back to tag him so he could start his run. No one blames us for messing up. No one blames you guys for being small," he assured them.

"It is okay to be sad and disappointed that you didn't win. Next time you might. Do you know what is important after a race of any kind whether you win or not?" Lawrence asked them.

Colleen and Henrietta looked at each other and shrugged, then looked back to Lawrence and shook their heads.

"No matter what happens in any game, other than having fun and trying your best, you should always be a good sport and show support for the others. And win or lose, be graceful about the outcome. If you win be humble, if you lose be a good sport. It is never fun playing with a sore loser or with a poor winner."

"You're right," said Colleen. "We have not been very good sports."

"Yeah," agreed Henrietta. "We have not even congratulated our friends for their hard work."

They both struggled to smile back, then Henrietta grinned widely. "It sounds like we are missing the celebration, by pouting over here." She said to Colleen. "Let's go congratulate our friends."

"You're right." Colleen agreed. "Thank you, Lawrence. I see I wasn't being a very good sport. Let's go see our other friends."

They thanked Lawrence and ran back to the rest of the friends, ready to be much better teammates and contestants.

They went back to the tree and were welcomed with laughter, hugs and a round of cheers.

ABOUT THE AUTHOR

Tif E. Boots wrote her first children's book as a birthday present for her daughter. Her characters soon demanded another adventure and became the series *Brutus and Friends*.

Many years later, Tif has been awarded:

2024 POTY Book Longlist Award for *Charlie's Tangle*.

2024 Literary Global Children's Book Finalist Award for *Scrump and Friends go for a Swim*.

2024 American Writing Awards Finalist for *Charlie and the Scavenger Hunt*.

Tif was raised in Marana, Arizona and was working concession stands at county fairs in Arizona and Michigan with her family until she graduated from Marana High School in 2000. She became a mother and correctional officer in 2004. She then moved to Nevada, Missouri with her family where she was blessed with her second daughter and fell into a career of nurse's assistant for Hospice.

Her books have been translated into Spanish, Gaelic, French, German, Italian, Dutch, and Portuguese.

Tif and her family relocated to Mulberry, Florida in 2017. In her free time Tif can usually be found on the water or at amusement parks spending time with family and friends and simply enjoying the life that God has blessed her with.

You may reach Tif through BootsBooks.net. She would love to hear from you.

ABOUT THE ILLUSTRATOR

Syranity Barker is an illustrator who has always had a love for art. She was born in Tucson, Arizona and eventually moved to central Florida where she graduated high school.

Syranity illustrated her love of drawing early in life; her family were great supporters of her passions and always made sure she had a variety of supplies and mediums. While she was still in high school, her work was entered in numerous art shows. She received the *City Commissioners Choice Award* for a mixed media portrait of her dog and has sold several pieces of her work.

Still fresh out of high school, Syranity works two jobs and illustrates professionally in her spare time. She is currently the in-house illustrator for *ShelteringTree.Earth Publishing* and also promotes herself as a free-lance artist.

Syranity enjoys singing, skating, spending time with her friends and family, and creating her own characters and writing backstories for them.

Syranity aspires to become an art teacher and share her passion for drawing and self-expression with others.

BRUTUS and the RELAY RACE

DISCUSSION GUIDE FOR SMALL GROUPS, CLASSES, AND INDIVIDUAL REFLECTION

DIRECTIONS: Write your answers on the lines. In the space below the lines, draw a picture explaining your answer.

1. Why was Charlie super excited?

_____

_____

_____

_____

2. How was Charlie shaking the nest?

_____

_____

_____

_____

3. Who decides to join Charlie when he greets his friends?

_____

_____

_____

_____

4. Why did they decide to find more friends?

_____

_____

_____

_____

5. Who overheard them say they needed more friends to play?

_____

_____

_____

_____

6. Why do Henrietta and Coleen stay at the tree?

_____

_____

_____

_____

7. Who comes to the tree while Henrietta and Coleen are waiting?

_____

_____

_____

_____

8. How many of the friends can you name?

_____

_____

_____

_____

9. Why does Twitter decide not to race? What does she do instead?

_____

_____

_____

_____

10. Do you think the teams were fairly balanced? Why or why not?

_____

_____

_____

_____

11. Would you choose to run against a clumsy friend if you thought it would help you?

_____

_____

_____

_____

12. What was the problem that Twitter saw with the sticks?

_____

_____

_____

_____

13. Do you think she was right to have them all try to run with them instead of just saying it was wrong?

_____

_____

_____

_____

14. What is the first drop point for the sticks?

_____

_____

_____

_____

15.What three critters run the first round?

_____

_____

_____

_____

16. Who trips on the way to the slide? How did that affect the outcome of the race?

_____

_____

_____

_____

17.What advantage does Charlie have when in front of the other runners?

_____

_____

_____

_____

18. How does Henrietta get down the hill?

_____

_____

_____

_____

19. Why did Henrietta and Colleen leave at the end of the race?

_____

_____

_____

_____

20. Why did Lawrence point out his own mistakes when he was talking to the younger animals?

_____

_____

_____

_____

SHELTERING TREE

Earth
Publishing
ShelteringTreeMedia.com

For more information,

to become one of our authors, translators,

or illustrators,

or to contact the author or illustrator:

ShelteringTreeMedia.com

www.ingramcontent.com/pod-product-compliance
Lightning Source LLC
Chambersburg PA
CBHW060752180626
46818CB00002B/541